This igloo book
belongs to:

....

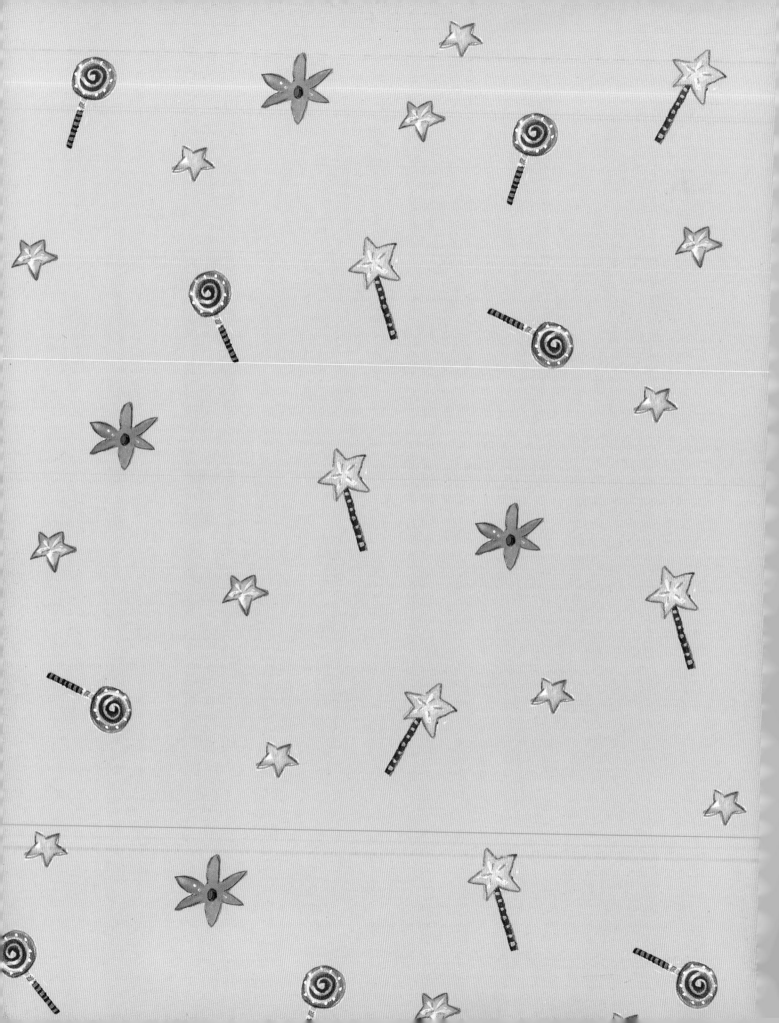

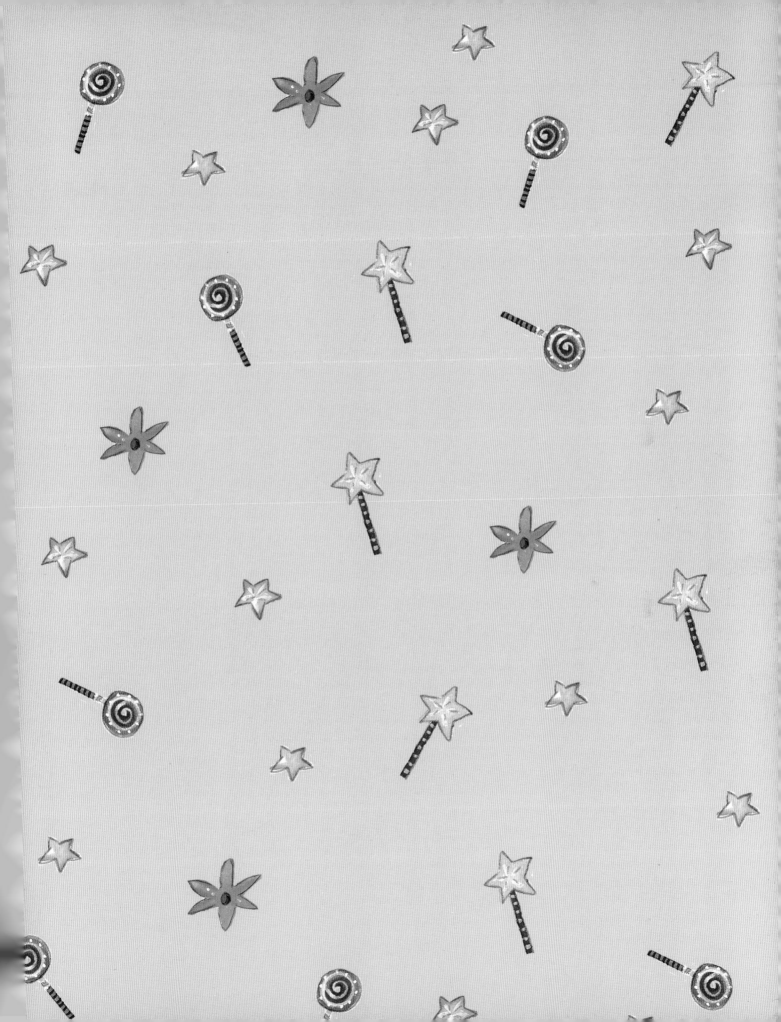

This edition published in 2019
by Igloo Books Ltd
Cottage Farm
Sywell
NN6 0BJ
www.igloo-books.com

Copyright © 2012 Igloo Books Ltd
Igloo Books is an imprint of Bonnier Books UK

0719 001.01
4 6 8 10 9 7 5 3
ISBN: 978-0-85780-432-7

Printed and manufactured in China

Tooth Fairy
Magic

igloobooks

Fairyland Forest was alive with the tinkle of tiny voices and the whisper of fluttering wings. It was the night of the fairy gathering, when fairies from all over the kingdom came to see Queen Isabella.

Everyone was there, except for Sparkle, the tooth fairy. Sparkle was collecting little teeth from girls and boys. Sparkle loved little children and adored her job, but it meant she was always late!

The forest suddenly went quiet. In a glittering flash of fairy dust, Queen Isabella appeared before the waiting fairies.

"Is everyone here?" she asked in a voice as sweet as honey and as light as a fairy's wing.

"Not quite," said one little fairy, stepping into the
fairy ring. It was Trixie, the problem-solving fairy.
"My best friend, Sparkle, is still hard at work. She is the
tooth fairy. She collects all the little teeth children lose
just before they get their grown-up teeth. She never knows
where she's going to find one, so she has to search every
nook and cranny, which takes a very long time."

When Trixie had finished speaking, an important-looking
fairy with a big stick tapped the ground three times.
"Let the meeting begin," she announced in a serious voice.

The first fairy to stand before Queen Isabella was Zoe,
the sewing fairy. She told everyone how she had made too
many fairy bags and didn't know what to do with them.

Then, while everyone puzzled over Zoe's problem, Ursula, the potion fairy, stood up.

"I've run out of sparkles," she said. "Without sparkles, I can't make fairy dust and without fairy dust there is no magic. I need to find something sparkly, pure and good to make more sparkles!"

Ursula had barely finished speaking, when a fairy suddenly flopped down in the centre of the fairy ring. It was a very tired and dirty-looking Sparkle.
She'd had a hard night searching for teeth beneath dusty beds and grimy floorboards.

"I heard that," she panted. "And I've got just the thing."
Sparkle reached into the fairy purse she was carrying
and pulled out something that sparkled in the moonlight.
"Baby teeth," she explained. "What could be more pure
and good? And just look at the sparkle!"

Everyone, including Queen Isabella, agreed that it was a perfect solution to Ursula's problem.

"And I've had an idea for Zoe's fairy bags," announced Trixie. "We can give them to all the little children to put their baby teeth in. Then, they can put the bag under their pillows. That way, Sparkle won't have to spend so much time searching for lost teeth."

Sparkle nodded her head enthusiastically. "I think it would be nice if we left the children a reward for their teeth, too," she added. "After all, without them we wouldn't have any fairy dust."

Queen Isabella was very pleased with the fairies' ideas. "Well done everyone," she said. When the meeting had finished, all the fairies fluttered and flew off into the forest.

The following day, before Sparkle flew off, the fairies gathered together to write letters to all of the little children in the world. As the fairies scribbled away, Sparkle told them what to write.

Dear . . . .
(write your own name here)

Don't worry if a baby tooth begins to wobble, then falls out. Put it in this little pouch and pop it under your pillow when you go to bed. While you are sleeping, I will take it away and leave you a coin in its place. Don't worry about the gap your missing baby tooth leaves, a brand new tooth will soon grow to fill it.

Lots of love,
Sparkle

The Tooth Fairy

When the fairies finished writing the letters, they all helped
Sparkle deliver them, along with the fairy bags.

From that day on, Sparkle was never late for anything again because her job was much easier.
All the little children put their baby teeth in their pouches and placed them under their pillows, where Sparkle could find them. Never again did she have to scramble under beds, or between floorboards. Sparkle was a very happy fairy indeed.

Sparkle wasn't the only one who was happy. Zoe was happy because all her lovely bags were being used and Ursula was happy because she had lots and lots of gorgeous sparkles for her fairy dust. Queen Isabella and the rest of the fairies were happy because they had lots of fairy dust to do magical things with.

But, best of all, the little children were happy because they knew that if they looked after their baby teeth, they would get a reward whenever one fell out!

"Goodbye!"